THE ADVENTURES OF TUCKER

BASED ON THE TRUE-LIFE EVENTS OF OUR LOVING DOG

TUCKER TIBERIUS "FLYBOY" THE FIRST

FOR SONNA

ANGUS MACDONALD
9/23/2020

ABOUT THE AUTHOR

"Angus MacDonald"

The name chosen by the author in loving memory of his grandfather. A kind and gentle man filled with love and an amazing inspiration to the young writer.

With a rich heritage in his past, coupled with a naturally endowed imagination, Angus seems to have an inexhaustible supply of material and ideas to share with his readers. Born, raised and still living in the Pacific Northwest with his family. Angus spends his days enjoying the company of his wife each day, days that typically start over coffee and a good game or 3 of crib. An adventurer at heart Angus began his life growing up as a commercial fisherman.

He loves to write both, stories and songs, hike, ski, swim, camp, scuba dive and has been a hang glider pilot.

CHAPTERS

Tucker meets Emma In –

"The Dog That Had To Have A Pillow"

"THE ADVENTURES OF TUCKER"

EMMA MEETS TUCKER
IN
"THE DOG THAT HAD TO HAVE A PILLOW"

1. TODAY IS THE DAY.

How exciting today seems.

Today is the day!

It seemed like forever to get to, today.

Waking up today was like waking up to a day filled with surprises, treats and gifts. You know, all the most important stuff in life. Only, that wasn't a good enough way to describe it because today is so much more exciting than that!

Why? Because today is the day, we're going to get our new puppy, Tucker.

That's right, today we will **finally** pick up Tucker!

Oh, how cute he looks in his pictures. All fluffy and soft looking. Like a little red fur ball with a cute little nose. Even his little black nose has a dash of red on it. Oh, he is so cute!

But the waiting has been so hard. At my age it seemed like a lifetime of waiting.

Finally, today has arrived and after a very long drive, we pull into the yard where Tucker was born and now my excitement is almost too much for me.

It's like my tummy is full of butterflies, fluttering around their favorite pink and purple flowers in the meadow down by the lake at home.

Oh! Here she comes. It's the puppy lady coming out of her house. I remember her from the picture's mom showed me.

I can see her, even though I can barely see up over the dash of the car to see out the front window.

Oh, my goodness, she has what looks like a little red furball in her arms.

Now, it seems like the butterflies are trying to swarm my tummy all at once!

Quickly, I undo my seatbelt and quickly get out of the car, just as mommy and daddy get out and start to say hello to the puppy lady.

The puppy lady says, "Well, this is Tucker" and she starts to hand that little red fluffy fur ball to mama.

Oh no!

WOW!

Tucker starts crying and whining like somebody stepped on him, but it really seems like he's saying,

"No! Don't give me to them! Please! I don't even know who they are! Please! No!"

It's clear to all of us how much Tucker loves the puppy lady and there's no doubt, Tucker has a heart filled with love to give to the right family and the right little girl, me, Emma.

After some instructions and collecting some toys, along with Tuckers snuggly baby puppy blanket, we say goodbye to the puppy lady and load into the car to start the long journey home.

Surprisingly, mommy puts that soft fluffy snuggly baby puppy blanket on **my** lap! Then she puts Tucker on the blanket and just like that, Tucker snuggles into his snuggly baby puppy blanket and with his head nestled on the curled-up edge of the blanket and falls fast asleep.

Of course, I don't think it was very long until I fell asleep too, just like baby Tucker.

2. END OF THE FIRST YEAR

Mmmmm!

I feel the warm touch of the sun on my face. It's such a soothing feeling when you're waking up in the morning to have that beautiful, warm sun on your face.

When my eyes finally first open, what do I see? As usual,
little Tucker, sound asleep right beside me.

He's sure a lot bigger than when we first got him though, almost a whole year ago now!

Tucker's so funny laying on his back with his little legs pointing up in the air and all stretched out.

He looks so comfy with his head up on my pillow. I never had a dog that wanted to sleep like that before but, that's Tucker. Tucker's not quite like most other dogs.

No, Tucker's not quite like most other dogs.

Tucker wakes up and I guess he knows that I'm awake too because, he suddenly gets up, stretch's, arching his back down and yawns then, he comes over to lie on my side of the bed snuggling up to me groaning and whining how happy he is to see me. Oh, does he ever groan and whine but in a very happy way. It's like I've been gone for a month instead of sleeping right next to him all night. Have you ever seen such a performance?

He's so funny and so loving.

No. Tucker's not quite like most other dogs.

Getting out of bed and into my warm, soft, fur lined slippers, I put on my favorite housecoat. Then, Tucker follows me out into the living room.

Mom is awake and sitting on the couch with her coffee. In his usual morning excitement Tucker runs and jumps up on the couch, and into mom's lap, (almost spilling her coffee), crying and groaning again because he's so happy to see her.

Like every other day, mom laughs at this crazy good morning hello. When Tucker is happy it's like he's smiling and he groans and his lips curl back showing his teeth just like a human smile.

No, Tuckers not quite like most other dogs.

It's like this every morning!

Tucker is such a loving little dog. Just as we thought he would be the first day we met him with the puppy lady so long ago.

Tucker is full of love.

After a few minutes, Tucker starts to settle down and like every other day, he suddenly decides he needs a nap. After all the excitement of the morning so far, seeing everyone for the first time in the day, a young dog needs a good rest.

So, Tucker jumps down to the floor and starts to turn circles around on the carpet to get comfortable. What's strange is when he lays down! He falls asleep and then wakes up. He gets up and does a couple more circles on the carpet. Then, he lays down again and tries to sleep. He looks a little uncomfortable and I don't know why. We've had dogs before that had no problems sleeping on the carpet like that but,

Tucker’s not quite like most other dogs.

After doing this for some time and then moving to another spot and another spot and yet another spot Tucker, jumps back on the couch where mom has all those pretty little decorative pillows. Then, using his nose and scratching up with his paws he starts tossing those pretty little pillows all over, including on the floor.

Mom says, "Tucker. What are you doing?" But what can she say when, once he has rearranged things to his liking, he lays his head down on a pillow and falls fast asleep?

Don't you think what he does is a little strange?

I wonder why he does it?

Mom wonders why?

What do you think?

At night when I go to bed, I try to get him to lay on the bed by my feet like a good dog. Tucker keeps trying to get up by the top of my bed where my pillow is and I send him back down where I want him to sleep by my feet.

After giving me his big sad eyes for a while, Tucker finally lays down by my feet and goes to sleep. I'm not sure why he gives me that sad look? I thought he liked sleeping with me.

As I fall asleep, I can feel him by my feet, on top of the covers, turning and switching spots. It almost seems like he can't get to sleep. Like maybe even on my soft comfy bed and laying on top of my big fluffy down comforter he still can't get comfortable.

Why does this happen?

What's the problem?

I wonder why?

What do you think?

I fall asleep wondering what is wrong?

When I open my eyes in the morning, there he is, sleeping right beside me like a happy baby puppy again, with his head up on **my** pillow!

I wonder why he's sleeping so well now.

What do you think?

3. FUN AT THE BEACH

What a beautiful day.

I love it here.

The smell of the salt air, the sand, the laughter and sounds of children running along the beach in the warm, midday sunshine.

Is there anything better than a day at the beach in the warm, beautiful sun?

Oh, my goodness!

Look at him!

Tucker is covered in sand!

What a mess!

Teaching him to swim has been so much fun, and he loves to chase sticks out into the water.

The tough part is trying to get them away from him again when he gets back to the beach. It's like he's saying, "I swam out and got it. It's my stick now"!

But even then, I can tell, he still wants me to chase him. I think it's his favorite game so of course, I play along and chase him. He loves it but, when he comes out of the water to lay in the sand and chew on his stick he gets covered with sand.

Between playing at the park or walking in the trails behind our house to, playing and swimming at the beach, Tucker loves it all! He is such a fun dog, and my very best friend.

He's amazing and so smart! Why, just yesterday I watched him pull open the door to my room with his nose when the door was barely open and there was barely enough room to get his nose in the crack so he could open it and get out.

Wow! How did he figure that out?

But then again, Tuckers not quite like most other dogs.

Oh look! He's lying on the sand sound asleep! He sure is sleeping good now.

I wonder why he's sleeping so good now?

What do you think?

Finally, dad says it's time to go back up to the cabin for lunch. After drying off in the sun and brushing the sand off ourselves, we walk up the sandy lane to the beach cabin.

Mom has lunch ready as always and a nice treat for Tucker.

After lunch, it's time for a good nap.

I lay down on the couch and Tucker tries to get up on the couch with me but, I tell him to lie down on his little bed on the floor.

I'm not sure why he looks sad? It looks like a comfortable bed! It’s a thick, soft mat made especially for dogs.

We got it for him because he didn't seem comfortable lying on the carpet and we wanted him to be comfortable. He lays down on it, but he doesn't look that comfortable.

I wonder why?

Mommy wonders why?

What do you think?

When I wake up from napping on the couch, Tucker is sound asleep on the floor. But he's not on his bed. He's sound asleep on the carpet. That's odd! I wonder why he fell asleep there? I wonder why he's sleeping so well now?

What do you think?

4. CHIPMUNK MADNESS

Well, we're on the way to visit our favorite camping spot today.

It's a beautiful sunny day even if it is too cold to camp. Pretty soon the snow will be all gone but today it's so sunny, mom and dad just wanted to go for a nice drive.

Along the way of course we'll probably get to go have lunch out and that'll be fun too. Of course, by now, Tucker has learned about riding in the car and he gets so excited when we say, “Car ride”.

Once we say, "Car ride", he follows us around barking and whining like he's saying, "Well. Come on. Are we leaving yet? Hurry up. Let's go. I thought we were going in the car. You said we were going in the car. Let's go."

First, we have to take Tucker out for a walk before we get into the car for the long drive to the campground. Then, we have to put his driving harness on so we can buckle him into the car safely for the drive.

After that we load his comfy bed into the back with the seat down on his side, so he'll hopefully have a sleep on the way and then we climb into the car, buckle up our seatbelts and head down the driveway.

Of course, it's not long before I get sleepy and Tucker looks tired too although he is still awake. He puts his head down on his bed but just can't seem to sleep.

It's quite warm in the car with the windows up and the heater on, even if it is almost freezing outside. So, I take off my coat and put it down beside Tucker on his bed. Suddenly Tucker turns around and putting his head down on my coat he falls fast asleep.

Wow! I wonder why he fell asleep so fast now?

Do you know why?

I fall asleep wondering why?

Suddenly there's a bump. I wake up and realize were turning into the campground. The drive seemed very short this time. Tucker is awake now too and he looks at me as if he's saying, "What's going on? Are we OK? Where are we?"

Dad stops the car at our favorite camp spot next to the river. I jump out while mom puts the leash on Tucker. He can sure swim, but mom says she doesn't want a wet Tucker today. Besides it's so cold I can make great long clouds of steam with my breath when I breathe out. I love doing that.

Can you do that too?

The camp is right beside the river where there's a great big pool for swimming in when we camp here in the summer. We think it the best campsite in the whole campground.

We stay for a bit and let Tucker run around to the end of his leash. Tucker tries to chase the little chipmunks that show up every few minutes spending as much time as they can in case more snow comes, collecting whatever they are collecting to make sure they have enough extra food to last through the last part of the winter. If they only knew that it would soon be spring.

The Chipmunks are so funny to watch. While they're gathering, sometimes they chase each other around like they're trying to steal food from each other. Whatever they're doing with each other its sure fun watching them. They make me laugh.

Wouldn't you laugh?

Dad brought some chairs and a propane fire pit, so we sit around the warm fire next to the river for a while enjoying the warmth of the fire and the sunny day. It's not so cold with the fire burning and Tucker starts to fall asleep. He has his little head up on his camping blanket on the ground and falls fast asleep.

Those chipmunks sure seem to be having fun while they gather their treats. It's like they play tag and games while they work. It's better than watching tv at home and everyone is laughing at the fun they seem to be having.

Suddenly, one of the chipmunks runs along a log right towards Tucker and jumps through the air almost. It lands on Tuckers back and jumps away again before Tucker can get up to see what hit him.

We were all laughing so hard I fell out of my chair. Tucker is looking around, but he can't figure out what happened because he didn't see the chipmunk scurrying away from him. I wonder if that was part of the game for the chipmunk. Have you ever seen anything so funny?

After laughing ourselves silly, we finally put everything back in the car, belt Tucker into his seat on his bed and start the drive to where were going to have our lunch out. I love going to have lunch there because they let dogs in so Tucker can come in with us.

Once we get our seats in the restaurant and sit down, I take my coat off and put it on the back of my chair. Tucker lays down under my chair to sleep. Like always, he sleeps, wakes up and turns around then sleeps again. Poor Tucker.

I wonder why he does that?

What do you think?

We sit for quite a while talking and enjoying the view of the beautiful snow-capped mountains out the windows.

After that we started talking about our favorite camping spot and how fun it will be as soon as it's warm enough to go for our first trip camping this year. Back to sleeping in the tent, swimming in the pool in the river, watching the crazy chipmunks run around and watching them try to sneak into our camp to steal treats. I guess they'll never figure out we leave the treats out where they can get them on purpose just so we can get a good look at them again.

I forget about Tucker while he sleeps.

When we get up to go, I look down and realize my coat has fallen and Tucker is sleeping on it with his head on my coat just like a,,,,,,,,,,,,,,,,,,,,,,,,,,,,,,

A PILLOW!

THATS IT!

I THINK I KNOW WHY HE CAN'T SLEEP!

Why he fell asleep with his head on the curled-up edge of the puppy blanket when we first picked him up from the puppy lady so long ago!

Why he can't sleep on the carpet and gets up on the couch making a mess out of mom's pretty little decorative pillows!

Why he can't sleep on his comfy flat bed on the floor!

Why he can't sleep on the foot of my bed!

Why he has his head up on my pillow when I wake up in the morning!

Why he can fall asleep on the beach with his head up on the
rolled-up edge of a beach towel!

Why he falls asleep on one of his favorite stuffy toys on the floor!

Why he can fall asleep with his head on my coat on the floor!

Why didn't I realize it before?

Why didn't mom?

Why didn't dad?

Do you know Why?

It's suddenly so obvious that I just have to laugh at all of us and most of all at, my silly little bestest of all friends in the whole wide world, Tucker.

Because Tucker's not quite like most other dogs.

No, Tucker is not quite like most other dogs but, Tucker is certainly,

"The dog that had to have a pillow."

I hope that you enjoyed this first visit with Tucker as much as I enjoyed writing it for you. Please don't worry too much because I assure you, the next adventure is already on the way.

This time, "The adventures of Tucker", are going to take us to,,,,,,,,,,,,,,,,,,,,,,,,,,,,,,,

"The Adventures Of Tucker"

Tucker Goes Camping

Imagine where he will go after that. Just imagine!

I do.

Angus MacDonald

The second book in the series will take tucker and Emma back to that crazy chipmunk infested campground where Tucker may finally get the opportunity to even the score with those sneaky little guys. Of course, there may also be some very tense moments as Tucker learns the power of the big creek while he learns to swim. The people and animals he meets on this adventure will certainly have children mesmerized and imagining their own adventures if they could only join Tucker and Emma on their journeys.

SIGNED WITH LOVE FROM TUCKER TO YOU.

www.ingramcontent.com/pod-product-compliance
Lightning Source LLC
LaVergne TN
LVHW070225110826
845147LV00003B/652

* 9 7 8 1 7 3 6 4 0 7 5 1 6 *